A Day at the Beach

Sarah Russell

Illustrated by Andy Rowland

It was a sunny day.
"Let's go to the beach," said Dad.

Mum drove to the beach.
They all got out of the car.

Ruby and Tom went for a swim.

Milo went for a swim, too.

Ruby and Tom played with the ball.

Milo played with the ball, too.

Ruby and Tom made a sand castle.

Milo wanted to help.

"Woof! Woof!" said Milo.
"Oh no!" said Tom.

“It is okay, Milo,” said Ruby.

They made a new sand castle.
Milo helped, too!